'When the
men were off
somewhere,
he would come
visiting their
wives more
solicitously than
any priest they'd
had before . . .'

GIOVANNI BOCCACCIO
Born 1313, Tuscany
Died 1375, Tuscany

Selection taken from Boccaccio's *Decameron*,
translated by Peter Hainsworth.

BOCCACCIO IN PENGUIN CLASSICS
The Decameron
Tales from the Decameron

GIOVANNI BOCCACCIO

Mrs Rosie and the Priest

Translated by
Peter Hainsworth

PENGUIN BOOKS

PENGUIN CLASSICS

UK | USA | Canada | Ireland | Australia
India | New Zealand | South Africa

Penguin Books is part of the Penguin Random House group of companies
whose addresses can be found at global.penguinrandomhouse.com.

This selection published in Penguin Classics 2015
003

Translation copyright © Peter Hainsworth, 2015

The moral right of the translator has been asserted

Set in 9.5/13 pt Baskerville 10 Pro
Typeset by Jouve (UK), Milton Keynes
Printed in Great Britain by Clays Ltd, St Ives plc

A CIP catalogue record for this book is available from the British Library

ISBN: 978-0-141-39782-5

www.greenpenguin.co.uk

Contents

Andreuccio da Perugia's Neapolitan adventures

I was told some time ago about a young man from Perugia called Andreuccio, the son of a certain Pietro and a horse-dealer by trade. Having heard that horses were trading well in Naples, he put five-hundred gold florins in his bag and went off there with some other merchants, never having previously been away from home. He arrived on a Sunday evening, about vesper time, got the necessary information from his innkeeper and was in the market square early the next morning. He saw a lot of horses, many of which met with his approval, and did a good deal of bargaining without being able to agree a price for any of them. But he was keen to show that he was there to do some buying and naively and imprudently pulled out his bag of florins several times before the eyes of people coming and going past him. It was while he was negotiating, with his bag in full view, that a young Sicilian woman walked past. She was very beautiful, but ready to give any man what he wanted for a small payment. He didn't see her, but she saw his bag and immediately said

1

to herself, 'Wouldn't I be a lucky one if that money were mine?' Then she went on her way.

There was old woman with her who was also Sicilian. As soon as she saw Andreuccio, she let the girl go on and hurried over to give him an affectionate hug. The young woman noticed and, without saying anything, stopped and waited for her on one side. Andreuccio, who had turned round and recognized the old woman, greeted her with great warmth. She promised to come and see him at his inn, but didn't keep him talking for too long just then and soon left. Andreuccio went back to his bargaining, though he made no purchases that morning. After seeing first the bag and then the intimacy with the old servant, the young woman began to wonder if she might get hold of some or all of the money. She asked a few cautious questions about who the young man was, where he was from, what he was doing there and how she came to know him. The old servant gave her all the information she wanted, almost in as much detail as Andreuccio might have supplied himself, being able to do this because she had spent a long time with his father first in Sicily and then in Perugia. She likewise told her where he was lodging and why he had come to Naples.

Once the young woman was fully informed about his family and their names, she had the basis for playing a clever trick that would bring her what she wanted. Back at her house she made sure that the old woman was busy all day so that she couldn't go and see Andreuccio. She had a much younger servant-girl to whom she had given a very good training in the sort of work she had in mind, and towards evening she sent her to the inn where Andreuccio was staying. When she arrived, she found him by chance standing alone in the doorway. She asked for Andreuccio and he said that he was the very man. At which she drew him to one side.

'Sir,' she said, 'there is a noble lady in this town who would appreciate a conversation with you, if you were so inclined.'

Andreuccio thought carefully for a moment when he heard this. He decided that he was a good-looking lad and deduced that this lady must have fallen for him, as if there were no other fine young men in Naples just then apart from himself. He quickly said that he was up for it, and asked where and when this lady wanted to have a talk with him.

The young servant-girl replied, 'She's waiting for you in her house, sir, whenever you feel like coming along.'

'Well, you lead the way and I'll follow on,' said Andreuccio immediately, with no thought of letting anyone in the inn know.

So the girl led him to the Sicilian woman's house, which was in a district called Malpertugio, a name meaning Bad Passage, which gives a clear idea of just how respectable a district it was. But Andreuccio, knowing nothing of this and quite unsuspecting, thought he was going to a most respectable house to see a lady of some standing, and

3

confidently followed the girl into the house. As they were climbing the stairs, she called out to her mistress, 'Here's Andreuccio', and he saw her appear at the top, waiting for him.

She was still young, with a full figure and a lovely face, and her clothes and jewellery were tastefully ornate. When Andreuccio was closer, she came down three steps towards him, her arms wide, and, flinging them round his neck, stayed like that for a while without saying a word, as if too overcome to speak. Then she tearfully kissed his forehead and said in a broken voice, 'O my precious Andreuccio, welcome to my house!'

Such a heartfelt reception amazed Andreuccio, and he replied quite dazed, 'Well, it's wonderful to meet you, my lady!'

After this she took him by the hand and led him into the main room, and from there, without saying another word, into her private chamber, which was redolent with the scents of roses, orange blossom and other flowers. Andreuccio noticed a splendid curtained bed, and an abundance of beautiful dresses arranged on hangers in the south Italian way, and many other fine and costly items. In his inexperience he was fully convinced by all this that the woman could be nothing but a great lady. Once they were seated together on a chest that was at the foot of her bed, she embarked on the following speech.

'I am quite certain, Andreuccio, that you are startled at being embraced and wept over by me in this way. After all, you don't know me and and may never have heard my name mentioned. But in a moment you are going to hear something which will perhaps amaze you even more. The fact is, I am your sister. And I can tell you that, since God has granted me the enormous grace of letting me see one of my brothers before I die – though of course I want to see all of you – I shall not die unconsoled. Perhaps you have never heard a word of this. So I shall happily tell you all about it.

'As I think you may have been told, Pietro – that is, your father and mine – lived for a long time in Palermo. Thanks to his native goodness and appealing character he gained the affections of those who came to know him and still has a place in their hearts. But, among those most attached to him, there was someone who loved him more than anyone else, and that was my mother, who was a noble lady and recently widowed. She loved him so much that she put aside all fears of her father and brothers and any concern for her honour, and entered into intimate relations with him. As a result I was born into the world and am now the person you see before you.

'A little later, when a reason arose for Pietro to return to Perugia, he left me, still a very little girl, with my mother. From everything I heard, he never gave me or her another thought. If he had not been my father, I would be very critical of him, considering the ingratitude he showed to my mother – and let's leave aside the love he should have felt for me his daughter, and not by a

5

servant-girl or some woman of easy virtue either. My mother was inspired by the truest form of love when, knowing nothing of who he was, she put herself and everything she had in his hands. But there you are. Wrongs of long ago are more easily criticized than put right.

'So he left me a little girl in Palermo. When I had grown into more or less the woman you see before you, my mother, who was a rich lady, married me to a man from Agrigento, an upstanding man of noble rank. Out of love for myself and my mother he moved to Palermo, and there, being very much on the Guelf side, he became involved in plotting with our King Charles. King Frederick got wind of the plot before any of our plans could be acted on, and so we had to flee Sicily just at the moment when I was expecting to become the finest lady there had ever been on the island. We took with us what few things we could – I mean few in comparison to all the possessions we had – and, leaving our lands and mansions behind, escaped to this city. We found King Charles very grateful. He partially compensated us for the losses we had suffered on his behalf. He gave us lands and houses, and he still gives my husband, your brother-in-law, a substantial pension, as you'll soon be able to see. So that is how I came to be here, and how, thanks to God's grace, though not at all to you, I now see you before me, my sweet brother.'

With this she clasped him to her again and kissed his forehead, still weeping tenderly.

She told her cock-and-bull story in a supremely coherent and convincing way, with not a hesitation or stutter. Andreuccio recalled that his father really had been in Palermo and he knew from his own experience what young men are like, and how prone they are to falling in love. What with the tender tears, embraces and decidedly unamorous kisses, he was convinced that what she said was more than true. When she finished, he made the following reply.

'My lady, you must not be shocked by my own amazement. To be candid, either my father for some reason of his own never spoke about you and your mother, or if he did speak of you, not a whisper reached my ears. So I had no more knowledge of you than if you had never existed. But it's all the more precious to me to have found you, my sister, in this place, because I'm here all alone and this was the thing I least expected. And to tell the truth, I can't imagine your not being precious to the grandest businessman I can think of, let alone to a small-scale merchant like myself. But please, explain one thing for me. How did you come to know I was here?'

'I was told this morning,' she replied. 'And the person who told me is a poor woman who spends a lot of time here with me, the reason being that, from what she says, she was with our father for a long time in both Palermo and Perugia. If it hadn't seemed to me more honourable for you to come here to what is your house than for me to come and see you at someone else's, I would have been with you ages ago.'

After this she started putting precise questions to him about his relatives, identifying each one by name. Andreuccio told her about them all, becoming more and more willing to believe what he should not have believed at all.

Since they kept on talking for a long time and it was very hot, she called for white wine and sweetmeats, and ensured that Andreuccio was duly served. He made to leave after this since it was now dinnertime, but she wouldn't allow it. Looking deeply distressed, she flung her arms round him, saying, 'Oh, poor me, I can tell I don't really matter to you! To think that you're here with a sister you've never seen before, in her house, where you should have come and stayed when you arrived, and you want to go off and have your dinner in an inn. No, you'll dine with me, and though my husband is not here, I'm very sorry to say, I'll do what little a lady is capable of to see you are treated with some degree of honour.'

Andreuccio could only come up with one reply.

'You do matter to me,' he said, 'as much as any sister should. But if I don't go, I shall keep them waiting for me for dinner all evening, which would be really churlish.'

'Lord in heaven,' she said, 'do you think I've nobody

in the house I can send to tell them not to expect you? Though you would be doing a finer thing, not to say your duty, if you sent a message to your friends inviting them to come and dine here. Then afterwards, if you were set on leaving, you and all the rest could go off in one big party.'

Andreuccio replied that he had no wish to see his friends that evening, and that, if this was how she felt, she should treat him as she pleased. She then made a show of sending a message to the inn telling them not to expect him for dinner. After this they talked on for a long time before sitting down to eat. They were served in a splendid fashion with a series of dishes, the woman cunningly prolonging the dinner well into the night. When they got up from the table, and Andreuccio expressed a desire to leave, she said that she could not possibly allow it. Naples was not a city for anyone to walk through at night, especially a stranger. She had sent a message to say he should not be expected for dinner and then she had sent another regarding where he was staying. He believed everything she said, and was delighted, in his deluded state, to stay on.

At her instigation conversation after dinner was prolonged and varied. Late into the night she left Andreuccio in her own chamber, with a young servant-boy to show him anything he needed, while she herself went off to another room with her maids.

It was very hot and as soon as he saw he was alone

Andreuccio removed his jacket and peeled off his leggings, which he left over the bedhead. Feeling nature calling him to lighten his stomach of the excess weight within it, he asked the servant where one did that sort of thing. The boy pointed to a door in a corner of the room.

'Go in there,' he said.

Andreuccio went insouciantly though the door. By chance he brought one of his feet down on a board, the other end of which was no longer attached to the joist on which it was resting. The result was that the board swung up in the air and then crashed downwards, taking Andreuccio with it. God was kind to him and he did himself no harm in the tumble, although he fell from a considerable height, but he was thoroughly covered in the horrible filth that the place was full of. To explain the arrangement in order to give you a clearer picture of what I've just said and what follows, two narrow beams had been fixed over the sort of narrow alleyway we often see separating two houses, with some boards nailed to them and a place to sit on fitted. It was one of these boards which had fallen with Andreuccio.

When he found himself down below in the alleyway, he was extremely upset at what had happened and began calling out to the boy. But, as soon as he had heard him fall, the boy had rushed to tell his mistress. She in her turn rushed into the bedroom, quickly looked to see if his clothes were there and found them. With them was the money, which, crazily, the ever suspicious Andreuccio always carried on his person. The Palermo tart, who now had what she had schemed for by turning into the sister of the visitor from Perugia, couldn't care less any more about Andreuccio. She went promptly over to the door which Andreuccio had passed through when he fell, and closed it.

When the boy didn't reply, Andreuccio started calling more loudly, but to no avail. He was now becoming suspicious and beginning, somewhat late in the day, to have an inkling of the trickery. He climbed on to the low wall separating the alleyway from the street and, once down on the other side, found his way to the door of the house, which he easily recognized. He stood there for a long time, vainly calling out and shaking and banging on the door. He could now see the full extent of his misfortune quite clearly, which reduced him to tears.

'Oh, poor me,' he began saying. 'How little time it's taken for me to lose five-hundred florins and a sister too!'

After a lot more of this he began again beating on the door and calling out. The result was that many people living nearby woke up and then, when the din became unbearable, got themselves out of bed. One of the lady's female servants appeared at a window, looking all sleepy, and called out in an irritated voice, 'Who's banging away down there?'

'Oh, don't you know me?' said Andreuccio. 'I'm Andreuccio, the brother of Lady Fiordiliso.'

The servant replied, 'My good man, if you've had too

11

much to drink, go and sleep it off and come back in the morning. I don't know anything about any Andreuccio or anything else you're gabbling on about. Do us a favour, please go away and let us get some sleep.'

'What?' said Andreuccio. 'Don't you really know what I'm saying? Oh, you must do. But if family relations in Sicily are like that and get forgotten as quickly as this, at least let me have back the clothes I left with you and I'll be glad to go on my way with only the Lord for company.'

The servant almost broke out laughing.

'Good man,' she said, 'I think you're dreaming.'

And even before she finished speaking, she was back inside with the window shut.

Andreuccio was now fully aware of his losses and the pain of the realization made him so angry it almost drove him wild. He could not recover what he had lost through words and he resorted to physical violence. He picked up a big stone and began savagely beating at the door again, only now with much more force. At this many of the neighbours who had been woken up and were out of their beds started thinking that he was some no-gooder who was inventing the whole palaver to bother the good woman. When the banging got too much for them, they started calling out from their windows, as if they were the neighbourhood dogs barking all together at some stray intruder.

'It's an outrage,' they said, 'coming at this hour of night to respectable women's houses with all this claptrap. Oh, go away, for God's sake, and please let us sleep. If you have anything to sort out with her, you can come back tomorrow. Just don't be such a blasted nuisance tonight.'

What they were saying perhaps encouraged the good Sicilian woman's pimp, who was inside the house, though he had not been seen or heard till now by Andreuccio. He came to the window and in his best horrible and savage voice called out loudly, 'Who's that down there?'

Andreuccio looked up when he heard this and saw someone who, so far as he could tell (which was not much), had the air of a man to be taken seriously. He had a thick black beard and was yawning and rubbing his eyes, as if he'd just awoken from deep sleep.

'I'm a brother of the lady of the house,' replied Andreuccio nervously.

The man did not wait for him to go on.

'I can't think,' he said in an even more intimidating voice than before, 'why I'm stopping myself from coming down there and giving you such a thrashing you won't ever move again. An irritating drunk of a donkey, that's what you must be, not letting anyone round here get any sleep tonight.'

With that he turned back inside and bolted the window.

Some of the neighbours knew what sort of a man he

13

was and whispered a few fearful words of advice to Andreuccio.

'For God's sake,' they said, 'go away, good man, don't get yourself murdered down there. Go away for your own good.'

Being already terrified by the ruffian's voice and appearance, Andreuccio saw every reason for accepting this advice, which he felt was motivated by simple goodwill. He was now as dejected as anyone could be and despaired of recovering his money. He set off towards the part of the city he had come from following the servant-girl earlier that day, aiming to get back to his inn, but with no idea of the way. Then, since the stench he could smell coming from him was disgusting, he decided to go towards the sea in order to wash himself down. But he turned leftwards and headed up a street called the Ruga Catalana, or Catalan Way. This was taking him to the higher part of the city, when he happened to see in front two figures coming towards him with a lantern. He was afraid they might be part of the official watch, or else just up to no good. He noticed an open building nearby and quietly crept in to try to avoid them. But it was as if they had been directed precisely to that spot. They too entered the building. One was carrying various tools round his neck, which he unloaded, and the two of them began looking the tools over and commenting on them.

At a certain point in their conversation, one of them said, 'What can it be? I can smell the worst stink I've ever smelt.' And then, lifting up the lantern a bit, they saw the miserable Andreuccio.

'Who's that there?' they asked, astounded.

When Andreuccio said nothing, they came over to him with the light and asked him what he was doing there in such a repulsive state. Andreuccio told them the whole story of what had happened to him. They guessed where it could have been and said to each other, 'It must have all happened at that villain Buttafuoco's.'

'My good lad,' said one of them, turning to Andreuccio, 'you might have lost your money, but you have plenty reason for praising the Lord that you happened to have that fall and then couldn't get back into the house. If you hadn't fallen, you can be sure that you'd have been murdered as soon as you dropped off to sleep, and then you'd have lost your life as well as your money. But what's the point of crying over it at this stage? You've as much chance of getting a penny back as of picking stars from the sky. You're likely to end up dead if that villain hears you've been blabbing away.'

Then, after some conferring together, they put a proposal to him.

'Look, we feel sorry for you,' they said. 'So, if you want to join us in a certain project we are en route to perform, we are of the definite opinion that your share of the profits will amount to much more than what you have lost.'

Andreuccio, in his desperate state, replied that he was ready and willing.

That day had seen the burial of a certain Archbishop of Naples called Messer Filippo Minutolo. He had been buried in elaborate finery with a ruby ring on his finger worth over five-hundred gold florins. The two of them had in mind to detach it. They explained the scheme to Andreuccio, who let greed override good sense, and the three of them set off.

Andreuccio was still giving off a strong smell as they proceeded towards the cathedral.

'Can't we find a way,' said one of the two at a certain point, 'for this companion of ours to have a wash somewhere to stop him stinking so horribly?'

'Yes,' said the other, 'we're near to a well now. It's always had a pulley and a big bucket. Let's go over and give him a quick wash.'

When they reached the well, they found the rope was there but the bucket had been removed. So they decided to tie Andreuccio to the rope and lower him into the well. Once at the bottom, he would wash himself, and then, when he had done, he would give the rope a shake and they would pull him up.

So they moved into action and lowered Andreuccio into the well. But it so happened that some of the night watch were feeling thirsty because of the heat and also because they had been chasing after someone. They were coming towards the well to get a drink when the other two saw them, and at once took to their heels, without any of the company coming after water seeing them.

Down in the well, Andreuccio, having finished washing, shook the rope a few times. The thirsty watchmen, who had now unstrapped their bucklers, their weapons and their surcoats, began pulling on the rope, believing that it was attached to a big bucketful of water.

As soon as Andreuccio saw he was near the rim of the well, he let go of the rope and grabbed hold of the rim in his hands. The sight was enough to terrify the watchmen, who immediately, without a word, let go of the rope and ran off as fast as they could. Andreuccio was profoundly startled. If he had not kept a firm hold, he would have fallen back into the well and perhaps have hurt himself badly, or even finished up dead. Once he was finally out of the well, he found the abandoned weaponry, which he knew his companions had not been carrying, and was even more amazed. Nervous, unclear what was going on, bemoaning his misfortune, he decided to take himself off without touching anything and wandered away with no idea of where he was heading. He was going along like this when he bumped into his two companions, who were coming back to pull him up out of the well. They were astonished and asked him who had actually done that. Andreuccio replied that he did not know, but gave them a full account of what had occurred and of what he had found by the well.

His companions realized what had happened and explained, laughing, why they had run away and who the people were who had pulled him up. Then, without

17

wasting any more words since it was already midnight, they all went off to the cathedral. They got in quite easily and reached the tomb, which was marble and very large. They used their irons to lift the cover, which was enormously heavy, raising it just enough for a single man to get inside, and then they propped it up.

When this was done, one of them asked, 'Who's going to go inside?'

'Not me,' said the other.

'Nor me either,' said the first. 'But let Andreuccio go in.'

'I'm not doing that,' said Andreuccio.

Both of them turned on him.

'What do you mean you won't go in?' they said. 'By God, if you don't go in, we'll give you a bashing round the head with one of these iron poles and that'll be the end of you.'

This put the wind up Andreuccio. He went inside, thinking to himself as he did so, 'These two are making me enter the tomb in order to trick me. When I've passed them everything and am getting myself out again, they'll be off and I'll be left with nothing.'

He decided first and foremost to pocket his own share. He remembered the precious ring he had heard them discussing and, as soon as he was in the tomb, he took it off the Archbishop's finger and put it on his own. Then he passed them the crozier, the mitre and the gloves and stripped the body down to the shirt, passing them each item, saying that was all there was. They protested that

18

the ring must be somewhere and told him to look every-where. He replied that he couldn't find it and pretended to go on looking, keeping them waiting for some time. But they were as canny as he was. They continued telling him to keep looking and then, picking their moment, they pulled away the prop supporting the lid of the tomb and ran off, leaving Andreuccio enclosed within. Anyone can guess how Andreuccio felt when he heard the lid fall.

He tried many times to push up the lid with his head and shoulders, but his efforts were useless. He was so overcome with the anguish of it all that he passed out, collapsing on the Archbishop's dead body. And anyone who had seen the two of them would have had difficulty deciding which was the more lifeless, the Archbishop or Andreuccio. When he came to his senses, he broke into a flood of tears, foreseeing that he could not avoid one of two ends. If no one came to open the tomb, he was doomed to die of hunger and the stink among the worms from the corpse. Or else, if people came and found him inside the tomb, he would be hung as a thief.

With these bleakly distressing thoughts going round in his head, he heard movement in the church and many people talking. They were, he gathered, going to do what he and his companions had already done. This sharply increased his terror. But when they had opened the tomb and propped up the lid, they began to argue about who should go inside, which none of them wanted to do. At last, after much dispute, a priest said, 'What are you frightened of? Do you think he's going to eat you? The dead don't eat people. I'll be the one to go in.' With this he leaned over the edge of the tomb, turned his head outwards and swung his legs inside in order to lower himself down. Andreuccio saw what was going on, jumped up and seized the priest by one of his legs and made as if to pull him down inside. When the priest felt himself being pulled, he let out an enormous shriek and scrambled out of the tomb as fast as he could. This terrified the rest of them. Leaving the tomb open, they took off as if they were being chased by a hundred thousand devils.

Seeing them go, Andreuccio clambered out of the tomb, happier than he could have hoped, and left the church by the way he had come in. It was almost daylight as he walked off, trusting to luck, with the ring on his finger. But he reached the seafront and finished up somehow at his inn, where he discovered that the merchants he had come with and the innkeeper had been worrying about him all night. He told them what had happened to him and they all opined that he should take the innkeeper's advice and leave Naples immediately. He quickly did so and returned to Perugia, with his funds now invested in a ring, after having set out to do some horse-trading.

Ricciardo da Chinzica loses his wife

There was once a judge in Pisa with more brains than muscle called Messer Ricciardo da Chinzica, who may have thought that what worked well with his studies would satisfy a wife too. Being very rich, he was able to devote considerable time and effort to searching for a good-looking young lady to marry, whereas, if he had been able to give himself the sort of professional counsel he gave to others, good looks and youth were just what he should have run away from. And he managed it: Ser Lotto Gualandi gave him one of his daughters in marriage. She was called Bartolommea and she was one of the best-looking and most fanciable girls in Pisa, though admittedly there aren't many there who don't look like hairy spiders. The judge took her home with great razzmatazz, and the marriage-feast was magnificent.

When he finally geared himself up for the actual consummation, he just about brought it off. But being scrawny, wizened and not exactly spunky, next morning he had to have a glass of fortified wine, some sweet biscuits and other pick-me-ups before he could re-enter the world of the living. The experience gave the judge a better idea of his capabilities than he had had before, and he began teaching his wife a calendar of saints' days of the kind that schoolboys pore over looking for holidays which might have been made in Ravenna. As he now showed her, there wasn't a day that wasn't a saint's day, or rather every day had a multitude of them. Reverence for these demanded, as he demonstrated on various grounds, that man and woman should abstain from acts of congress. Then he threw in fasts, the four Ember days, evening vigils for the Apostles and hundreds of other saints, Fridays, Saturdays, the Lord's Day, the whole of Lent, certain phases of the moon and endless other special cases, no doubt assuming that the breaks from court-work he enjoyed from time to time applied just as much to women in bed. So this was how he managed things for a long time, with his wife becoming seriously depressed from being given at best a monthly treat, while he always kept a watchful eye on her just in case someone else gave her lessons about working days like the ones he had given her about saints' days.

Since the next summer was very hot, Messer Ricciardo found himself wanting to go off to a beautiful property he had near Monte Nero, where he could relax and enjoy the air for a few days. With him he took his lovely wife. To give her some entertainment while they were there, one day he organized a fishing trip. The two of them sailed out on small boats to watch the spectacle, he on one with the fishermen, she on the other with some ladies. They were so captivated that they drifted several miles along the coast almost without realizing it. But while they were gazing in rapt attention, a sloop suddenly came on the scene, belonging to Paganino da Mare, a celebrated corsair of the time. Once it sighted the boats, it set a course straight for them. They were unable to get away fast enough and Paganino caught up with the boat with the ladies in it. As soon as he laid eyes on Messer Ricciardo's beautiful wife, he stopped wanting any other booty, and whisked her into his sloop under the eyes of her husband, who was now on shore, and sailed away.

It doesn't take much to imagine how upset the judge was by the sight, given that he was so jealous he was fearful of the very air she breathed. In Pisa and elsewhere, he started fruitlessly complaining about the criminal behaviour of corsairs, but without discovering who had carried off his wife, or where they had taken her.

When Paganino took in how beautiful she was, he felt that he was on to a good thing. Not having a wife, he thought he might hang on to her permanently and began gently soothing her tears, which were copious. He had long ago thrown away saints' calendars and forgotten all about feast-days and holidays. That night he consoled her with some action, on the grounds that words had not helped much during the day. His consolations were so effective that the judge and his rules had gone entirely out of her head before they reached Monaco, and she began to have the time of her life with Paganino. And once he had got her there, he not only consoled her day and night, but honoured her as his wife.

After a while Messer Ricciardo got wind of the whereabouts of his good lady. Ardently desiring to do something and believing that no one else could manage to do what needed to be done, he made up his mind to go and get her himself, being prepared to pay out any amount of money to recover her. So he set to sea and sailed to Monaco. Once there he caught sight of his wife, and she caught sight of him, as she reported back to Paganino that evening, also informing him what his intentions were. When Messer Ricciardo saw Paganino the next morning, he went up to him and quickly started an easy, friendly conversation with him, while Paganino pretended all the while not to recognize him and waited for him to get to the point. When he judged the moment had arrived, deploying his best abilities in the most ingratiating way possible, Messer Ricciardo disclosed the reason why he had come to Monaco, begging Paganino to take as much money as he wanted and give him back the lady.

'Sir,' replied Paganino with a cheerful expression on his face, 'you are very welcome here. My reply in brief is as follows: it is true I have a young woman in my house, though I don't know whether she's your wife or someone else's. I don't know anything about her except what I've gathered from her during her stay with me. If you are her husband as you say, I'll take you to her since you seem to me a likeable gentleman and I'm sure she'll recognize you very well. If she says that the situation is as you say and wishes to go away with you, then, since I do love a likeable man such as you, you can give me the amount you yourself decide on for a ransom. But if the situation should be different, it would be indecent for you to try to take her from me, since I've got youth on my side and can hold a woman in my arms as well as any man, particularly one who is more attractive than any other girl I've ever seen.'

'She certainly is my wife,' said Messer Ricciardo, 'as you'll soon see if you take me to where she is. She'll fling her arms round my neck straight away. So I won't ask for the terms to be different from those you've thought up yourself.'

'Let's go then,' said Paganino.

So they walked off to Paganino's house and went into a reception-room, from where Paganino sent for her. She appeared from a chamber properly and neatly dressed and went over where Messer Ricciardo was waiting with Paganino. There she addressed only the sort of remarks to Messer Ricciardo that she might have made to any other stranger who had come with Paganino to his house. The judge, who was expecting to be given a rapturous welcome, was amazed.

'Could it be,' he began to wonder, 'that depression and my protracted sufferings ever since I lost her have altered me so much that she doesn't recognize me?'

'Lady,' he said, 'taking you fishing has cost me dear. No one has suffered as much as I have since I lost you, and here you are seeming not to recognize me, given the unfriendly way you're talking. Can't you see that I'm your Messer Ricciardo, who's come here to pay whatever sum is demanded by this fine gentleman in whose house we find ourselves, so that I can have you back and take you away from here? He's being kind enough to restore you to me for a sum of my own choosing.'

The lady turned to him and gave him a faint smile.

'Are you addressing me, sir?' she asked. 'You should check you've not mistaken me for somebody else. As far as I'm concerned, I don't recall ever seeing you before.'

'It's you who should check what you're saying,' said Messer Ricciardo. 'Look at me properly. If you're willing to do a little serious recalling, you're bound to see that I'm your very own Ricciardo da Chinzica.'

'Sir, you'll forgive me,' said the lady, 'but it's not as right and proper as you imagine for me to give you a lengthy looking-over. All the same, I've looked at you enough to know that I've never seen you before.'

Messer Ricciardo imagined that she was acting in this way out of fear of Paganino and did not want to admit to knowing him in his presence. So, after a few moments, he asked Paganino if he would be so kind as to let him speak with the lady alone in her chamber. Paganino said that he was happy to do so, on condition that he didn't start kissing her against her will. Then he told the lady to go with him into the chamber, listen to what he wanted to say and give him whatever reply she felt like.

Once the lady and Messer Ricciardo were in the chamber by themselves and had sat down, Messer Ricciardo began entreating her. 'Oh, heart of my life, my own sweet soul, my one hope, don't you recognize your Ricciardo, who loves you more than he loves himself? How can it be? Have I altered so much? Oh, lovely darling girl, at least give me a little look.'

The lady broke out laughing and wouldn't let him go on. 'You are very well aware,' she said, 'that I've not such a bad memory that I don't know you are Messer Ricciardo da Chinzica, my husband. But you made a poor show of knowing me as long as I was with you. You're not as wise as you want people to think you are, and you never were. If you had been, you really should have had the wit to see that I was young, fresh and frisky, and then have consequently acknowledged that young ladies require something else apart from food and clothing, though modesty forbids them to spell it out. But you know how you managed all that.

'You shouldn't have married, if you liked studying law more than studying your wife. Not that I thought you were much of a judge. You seemed more like a crier calling out holy days and feast-days, you knew them so well, not to mention fast-days and overnight vigils. Let me tell you that if you had given as many days off to the labourers working your lands as you did to the one who should

27

have been working my little plot, you'd not have harvested one grain of corn. By chance I've met with this man here, chosen by God, because he shows a compassionate concern for my young age. And I stay with him in this chamber, where no one knows what a feast-day is. I mean those feast-days that you celebrated one after another, piously serving the Lord in preference to the ladies. Saturdays don't pass through that door, neither do Fridays, vigils, Ember days or Lent, which just goes on and on. No, it's all work, day and night, banging away all the time. As soon as the bell rang for matins this morning, there we were back at it, doing the same job again and again, as I know very well. So I intend to stay and work with him while I'm young, and keep feast-days and penances and fasts for when I'm old. Get out of here as soon as you can and good luck to you. Go and keep your saints' days as much as you like without me.'

Messer Ricciardo's distress at hearing her speak like this was unbearable.

'Oh, sweet soul of mine,' he said, when he realized she had finished, 'what are you saying? Aren't you bothered at all about your family's honour or your own? Do you want to stay here as this fellow's tart, living in mortal sin, rather than be my wife in Pisa? He'll get fed up with you and throw you out in total disgrace. But I'll always hold you dear and you'll always be the lawful mistress of my house, even if I didn't want to be your husband. Oh, please listen. Are you going to let this unbridled, immoral lust make you forget your honour and forget me, when I love you more than my very life? Please, my dear love, don't say things like that any more, just come away with me. Now that I know what you want, I'll really make an effort from now on. So, sweetheart, change your mind, come away with me. I've been so miserable since you were carried off.'

'Now that there's nothing to be done about it,' said the lady, 'I don't see how anyone apart from me can be squeamish over my honour. I just wish my family had been a bit more squeamish when they gave me to you! But since they didn't bother about my honour then, I don't intend to bother about theirs now. If my sin's a mortar one, I'll stay stuck in it like a pestle. So don't you worry about me. And what's more, let me tell you that I feel like Paganino's wife here, while I felt like your tart in Pisa, what with lunar charts and geometric squarings having to align your planet and mine, while here Paganino has me in his arms all night, squeezing me, biting me, and the state he leaves me in God alone can tell you. Then you say you'll make an effort. Doing what? Waiting for something to happen? Straightening it by hand? I can tell you've turned into a redoutable knight since I saw you last! Go on, do your best to come to life. But you can't manage it. I don't think you belong in this world, you look such a wasted, miserable little wimp. And another thing. If he leaves me – which I don't think he's inclined to do as long I want to stay with him – I've no intention of ever coming back to you. Squeeze you till you squeaked, and you still wouldn't produce a spoonful of sauce. That meant that when I was with you I just lost out and paid out. I'm after better returns somewhere else. To go back to where I started, I tell you there are no feast-days and no vigils here, where I intend to stay. So leave as quickly as you can, and the Lord be with you. If you don't, I'll start shouting that you're forcing yourself on me.'

Messer Ricciardo saw that the game was up, recognizing there and then the folly in marrying a young wife without the appropriate wherewithal. He left the chamber in a saddened, suffering state and spoke a lot of waffle to Paganino, which got him nowhere. In the end, he left the lady and returned empty-handed to Pisa. The blow affected his mind and, when he was walking around the city, if someone greeted him or asked him a question, he would only reply, 'A horrid hole hates a holy day.'

It wasn't long before he died. When Paganino heard, knowing how much the lady loved him, he took her as his lawful wedded wife. Thereafter, with no thought for holy days or vigils or Lent, they worked their patch as much as their limbs would let them, and had a wonderful time together.

Mrs Rosie and the Priest

So, to begin, there's a village not far from here called Varlungo, as every one of you knows or will have heard from other people. It had once a valiant priest, a fine figure of a man who served the ladies well. He was not much of a reader, but every Sunday he would spout wholesome holy verbiage beneath the churchyard elm to refresh the spirits of his parishioners. When the men were off somewhere, he would come visiting their wives more solicitously than any priest they'd had before, sometimes bringing religious bits and pieces, holy water or candle-ends into their houses, and giving them his blessing.

Now among the women of the parish he took a fancy to, there was one he particularly liked, called Mrs Rosie Hues. She was the wife of a labourer by the name of Willy Welcome, and she really was a lovely ripe country-girl, tanned, sturdy, with lots of grinding potential. She was also better than any girl around at playing the tambourine, singing songs like 'The water's running down my river', and dancing reels and jigs, when she had to, waving a pretty little kerchief in her hand. With all these talents, she reduced the good priest to a quivering wreck. He would wander round the village all day trying to catch sight of her. When he realized she was in church on a Sunday morning, he would launch into a Kyrie or a Sanctus and struggle to come over as a virtuoso singer, though he sounded more like an ass braying, whereas, when he didn't see her there, he barely bothered to sing at all. All the same, he was clever enough not to arouse the suspicions of Willy Welcome or any neighbours of his.

From time to time, he would send Mrs Rosie presents in an effort to win her over. Sometimes it was a bunch of fresh garlic, since he grew the best in the region in a vegetable garden he worked with his own hands, sometimes it was a basket of berries, and now and then a bunch of shallots or spring onions. When he saw his chance, he would give her a hurt look and mutter a few gentle reproaches, while she acted cold, pretending not to notice, and looking all supercilious. So the estimable priest was left getting nowhere.

Now it happened one day that the priest was kicking his heels in the noontime heat out in the countryside with nothing much to do, when he bumped into Willy Welcome driving an ass loaded up with a pile of things on its back. He greeted him and asked him where he was going.

'To tell the truth, Father sir,' replied Willy, 'I'm off to town on a bit of business. I'm transporting these materials to Mr Notary Bonaccorri da Ginestreto to get him to aid and assist with a fiddle-faddle on the legal side that the assessor is officializing to put the whole house in order at last.'

'That, my son, is a good thing to do,' said the priest, full of glee. 'Go with my blessing and come back soon. And if you should happen to see Lapuccio or Naldino, don't let it slip your mind to tell them to bring me those straps for my threshing flails.'

Willy said he would do that and went off towards Florence, while the priest decided the time had come for him to go and try his luck with Rosie. He strode out vigorously and did not stop until he reached her house. He went in, calling out, 'God be with us! Is anyone here?'

Rosie was up at the top of the house. Hearing him, she shouted, 'Father, you're very welcome. What are you doing all fancy free in this heat?'

'God help me,' said the priest, ' I've come to spend a little time with you, having just met your man on his way to town.'

Rosie was downstairs by now. She sat and began cleaning some cabbage seeds her husband had sifted out a short time before.

'Well, Rosie,' said the priest, 'must you go on being the death of me like this?'

Rosie began to laugh.

'Well, what am I doing to you?' she said.

'You're not doing anything to me,' said the priest, 'but you don't let me do what I'd like to do to you, which is love my neighbour as God commanded.'

'Oh, get on with you,' said Rosie. 'Do priests do things of that sort?'

'Yes,' said the priest, 'and better than other men. And why shouldn't we? I tell you, we do a much, much better job. And do you know why? It's because we let the pond fill up before the mill starts grinding. And truly I can give you just what you need, if you'll only stay quiet and let me do the business.'

'What do you mean, just what I need?' said Rosie. 'You priests are all tighter-fisted than the devil himself.'

'I don't know,' said the priest. 'Just ask me. Maybe you want a nice little pair of shoes, or a headscarf, or a pretty woollen waistband, or maybe something else.'

'That's all very well, Brother Priest,' said Rosie. 'I've enough of that stuff. But if you're that keen on me, you can do me a particular favour, and then I'll do what you want.'

'Tell me what you're after and I'll be glad to do it,' said the priest.

'I have to go to Florence on Saturday,' said Rosie, 'to give in the wool I've been spinning and get my spinning wheel mended. If you let me have five pounds (which I know you've got), I'll get the pawnbroker to give me back my purple skirt and the decorated Sunday belt I wore when I got married. You know not having it has meant I can't go to church or anywhere respectable. And after that I'll be up for what you want for evermore.'

'God help me,' said the priest, 'I haven't the money on

me. But trust me, I'll make sure you have it before Saturday.'

'Oh yes,' said Rosie, 'you're all great at making promises. And then you don't keep any of them. Do you think you can treat me the way you treated Nell the Belle, who was left with just a big bass tum to play with? You're not going to do the same to me, by God. She ended up on the game because of you. If you haven't got it here, go and get it.'

'Oh, please,' said the priest, 'don't make me go all the way back to the house. You can tell my luck is up, and there's no one about. It could be that when I came back someone would be here to get in our way. I don't know when it might next stand up as well as it's standing up now.'

'That's all very fine,' she said, 'but if you're willing to go, go. If not, you'll just have to manage.'

He saw that she was only going to agree to his wishes when a contract was signed and delivered, whereas he was hoping for a bit of free access.

'Look,' he said, 'you don't believe I'll bring you the money. What about if I leave you this blue cape of mine as a guarantee? It's a good one.'

Rosie gave him a haughty look.

'This cape,' she said, 'how much is it worth?'

'What do you mean, how much is it worth?' said the priest. 'Let me tell you it's Douai cloth, double ply, maybe triple ply, and there are even people here who say it's got some foreply in it. I paid seven pounds at Lotto's second-hand clothes shop less than two weeks ago. It had five shillings knocked off, so it was a bargain, according to Bulietto d'Alberto, who you know is a bit of an expert in blue cloths.'

'Oh yes?' said Rosie. 'God help me, I'd never have believed it. But give it to me first.'

The good priest, who was feeling hard-pressed by his loaded weapon, unfastened his cape and passed it over.

'Well, Mr Priest,' she said, when she'd put it away, 'let's go down here to the shed. It doesn't get visitors.'

So off they went. And there he covered her in the sloppiest kisses in the world, introduced her to God's holy bliss and enjoyed himself generally with her for a good while. He finally left in the uncaped state priests normally appear in only at weddings and went back to the church.

There he reflected how all the candle-ends he picked up from his parishioners in the course of a year weren't worth half a fiver, and felt he had made a mistake. Now regretting leaving the cape behind, he started thinking about how to get it back at no cost to himself. Since he was quite crafty-minded, he figured out a good way of doing so. And it worked.

The next day being a feast-day, he sent the son of a neighbour of his to Rosie Hues's house, with a request for her to be so kind as to lend him her stone mortar, since Binguccio del Poggio and Nuto Buglietti were dining with him that morning and he wanted to make a sauce. Rosie sent it back with the boy. When it got to round lunchtime, the priest guessed Willy Welcome and Rosie Hues would be eating. He called his curate and said to him, 'Pick up that mortar and take it back to Mrs Rosie. Tell her, "The Father is immensely grateful and would like to have back the cape the boy left with you as a guarantee."'

The curate went to Rosie's house with the mortar and found her with Willy at the table eating their meal. He set down the mortar and gave them the priest's message.

Rosie was all set to give her reply to this request for the cape. But Willy's brow darkened.

'So you need guarantees from our estimated father, do you?' he said. 'I swear to Christ, I could really give you a clout up the bracket. Go and fetch it right now, and get yourself cancered while you're at it. And watch out for him wanting anything else of ours. He'd better not be told no, whatever it is. Even if it's our donkey, our donkey he gets.'

Rosie got up grumbling to herself and went over to the linen-chest. She took out the cape and passed it to the curate.

'You must give that priest a message from me,' she said, 'Say, "Rosie Hues vows to God that you'll never again be sauce-pounding in her mortar. That last time you didn't do yourself any credit."'

The curate went off with the cape and relayed Rosie's message to the priest, who burst out laughing.

'You can tell her next time you see her,' he told him, 'that if she won't lend out the mortar, I won't lend her the pestle. The one goes with the other.'

Willy believed that his wife had spoken as she did because he had told her off and gave the matter no further thought. But coming off worst made Rosie fall out with the priest, and she refused to speak to him until the grape-harvest, when he terrified her by threatening to have her stuffed into the mouth of the biggest devil in hell. She made her peace with him over fermenting must and roasting chestnuts, and after that the two of them had a good guzzle together on various occasions. To make up for the five pounds, the priest had her tambourine re-covered and a dinky little bell attached, which made her very happy.

Patient Griselda

Years ago a young man called Gualtieri inherited the marquisate of Saluzzo as the eldest son of the family. Being unmarried and childless, he spent all his time hunting birds and beasts, without giving a thought to marriage or future offspring. He should have been considered a very wise man, but his subjects disapproved. They kept begging him to get himself a wife so that he should not die without an heir and they should not be left without a lord. They kept offering to find him one with a suitable father and mother, who would satisfy their hopes and who would make him very happy.

Gualtieri's response was as follows: 'My friends, you are forcing me into something I had been completely set on never ever doing, given how difficult it is to find someone with the right character and habits, how plentiful are the inappropriate candidates, and how hard life becomes for the man who ends up with someone he doesn't get on with. You claim you can tell the daughters' characters from how the fathers and mothers behave, and argue on that basis that you can provide me with a wife I'll be pleased with. That is rubbish. I don't see how you can know the fathers properly, or the mothers' secrets for that matter. Besides, even if you could, daughters are very often unlike their fathers and their mothers. But since you like the idea of tying me up in these chains, I'll try to satisfy you, and, in order not to end up blaming anyone but myself if things should go wrong, I want to do the finding myself. But I tell you that if you don't honour and respect whoever I choose, you'll learn to your cost how hard it's been for me to take a wife against my will, just because you begged me to.'

His valiant subjects replied that they would be happy just so long as he could bring himself to get married.

Gualtieri had been impressed for a good while by the behaviour of a poverty-stricken young woman from a village near his family home. Since he also judged her to be beautiful, he calculated that life with her could be very pleasant. He looked no further and made up his mind to marry her. He had the father summoned and entered into an agreement with this complete pauper to take the girl as his wife.

That done, he called together all his friends in the area he ruled.

'My friends,' he said to them, 'you have been eager for me to make my mind up about a wife for some time. Well, I have made a decision, more out of wanting to comply with your wishes than from any desire to be married on my part. You know what you promised me – that is, to be content with the woman I chose, whoever she was, and to honour her as your lady. The time has come when I am about to keep my promise to you, and when I expect you to keep yours to me. I have found very near here a young woman after my heart. I intend to make her my wife and to bring her into my house in a few days. So arrange for the marriage-feast to be a fine one and to give her an honourable welcome. In that way I shall be able to say I am happy with how you have fulfilled your promise, and you will be able to say the same about me.'

His trusty subjects all replied that they were happy with this and that, no matter who she was, they would treat her as their lady and would honour her as such in every way. Then they all set about organizing a suitably grand and joyous celebration. And Gualtieri did his part too, arranging for a sumptuous and splendid marriage-feast, to which he invited a multitude of friends, relations, great nobles and other people from the surrounding area. In addition he had beautiful, expensive dresses made to fit a young woman who, he judged, had the same measurements as the girl he had decided to marry. Not only that, but he ordered belts, rings and a lovely, costly tiara, plus everything else a new bride should have.

Soon after sunrise on the day appointed for the wedding, Gualtieri mounted his horse, and all those who had come to honour him did the same. Everything needed was now in order, and he called out, 'Gentlemen, it is time to go for the new bride.'

After which he set off along the road to the village with the whole company. When they reached the girl's father's cottage, they found her hurrying back from the spring with some other women in the hope of catching sight of Gualtieri's bride. When he saw her, he called out to her by her name – that is, Griselda – and asked her where her father was.

'My lord,' she replied bashfully, 'he is in the house.'

Gualtieri dismounted and, telling everyone to wait, entered the poor cottage. Inside he found the father, a man called Giannucolo, to whom he said, 'I have come to make your Griselda my wife, but first I want to learn something from her own lips in your presence.'

What he asked her was whether, when he took her as his wife, she would do everything she could to please him, would not be upset by anything he might say or do, and would be obedient, together with many other questions of this sort. She replied yes to everything. Then Gualtieri took her by the hand and led her outside, where, in the presence of his whole company and everyone else, he had her stripped naked. He ordered the clothing he had had made to be brought and immediately had her dressed, and shoes put on her, and a tiara placed on her hair, unkempt though it was. Everyone was amazed.

'Gentlemen,' he said, 'this is the person I intend should be my wife, if she wishes to have me for her husband.'

Then he turned to her, standing there bashful and

awkward, and said, 'Griselda, do you want me for your husband?'

'Yes, my lord,' she replied.

'And I want you for my wife,' he said.

With that, before everyone present, he formally married her. Then he had her set on a charger, with attendants to do her honour, and took her home. The marriage-feast was grand and fine, and the festivities no different from what they would have been if he had married the daughter of the king of France.

The young wife's character and behaviour seemed to change with her change of clothing. As I said earlier, she had a lovely face and figure. And now to her natural good looks she added enough charm, attraction and refinement to make you think she could not possibly have been Giannucolo's daughter and a shepherd-girl, but the daughter of some noble lord. Everyone who had known her before was astounded. What is more, she was so ready to obey and serve her husband that he considered himself the most contented and satisfied man in the world. She was similarly so gracious and kindly towards her husband's subjects that every one of them loved her wholeheartedly and spontaneously honoured her in every way, asking God in their prayers to give her health, prosperity and greater glory still. If they used to say that Gualtieri had acted ill-advisedly in taking such a wife, now they said he was a paragon of wisdom and insight, arguing that no one else could have perceived the exceptional virtues concealed beneath the poverty of her peasant dress. All in all, before much time had passed, she had people speaking of her good qualities and virtuous deeds throughout the marquisate and beyond, and completely turning round any negative comments about her husband that had been made when he married her.

She had not been with Gualtieri very long when she became pregnant, and in due course she gave birth to a little girl, much to Gualtieri's delight. But a little later a strange idea came into his head. He felt a need to test her patience by inflicting unbearable torments on her over a prolonged period of time. First of all he made cutting remarks, and gave an impression of being angry with her. He said that his men were badly put out by her low-class origins, all the more now that she was having children. The girl-child was a particular source of resentment, and they wouldn't stop muttering about her.

When his lady heard this, she kept her composure and gave no sign of being thrown off the virtuous course she had set herself.

'My lord,' she said, 'treat me in the way that most accords with your honour and your happiness. I shall be content with anything. I am aware I'm less than they are and that I didn't deserve the honour you have had the generosity to bestow on me.'

Her response was warmly received by Gualtieri, who recognized that any honour that he or anyone else had paid her had not made her feel in the slightest bit superior.

A little while later, after giving his wife the general impression that his subjects couldn't stand the little girl she had borne him, he had a word with one of the household staff and sent him to her. The man addressed her with a distressed air.

'My lady,' he said, 'I am obliged to do something my lord commands me to do, if I do not wish to die. He has ordered me to take this daughter of yours and . . .'

He stopped there. Hearing his words and seeing his face, the lady recalled what her husband had been saying and deduced that he had orders to kill the child. She quickly took her from her cradle, kissed her and blessed her. For all the immense pain in her heart, she again kept her composure and put the child in the man's arms.

'Take her,' she said, 'and carry out to the letter what your lord and mine has ordered you to do. Only do not leave her for animals and birds to devour, unless he told you to.'

The servant took the child away and passed on what his wife had said to Gualtieri, who was astounded by her constancy. He then sent the servant off with the child to a female relative of his in Bologna, with a request to bring her up and educate her with the utmost care, but not to let anyone know whose daughter she was.

The next thing to happen was that the lady became pregnant again. In due course she gave birth to a male child, which pleased Gualtieri immensely. But what he had done already was not enough for him. His criticisms became sharper and sharper, and one day, his face contorted with rage, he said this to her:

'My lady, ever since you had this boy child, I haven't been able to live with these men of mine. They are bitterly against some grandson of Giannucolo ending up their lord after me. If I don't want to be hounded out of here, I'm afraid I'm going to have to do what I did the other time, and then in the end I'm going to have to leave you and take another wife.'

The lady heard him out without flinching.

'My lord,' was all she replied, 'think only of contenting yourself and following your own inclinations, and don't worry at all about me. Nothing matters to me except whatever I see pleases you.'

A few days later Gualtieri sent someone for his son, much as he had done as regards his daughter. After a similar show of having him murdered, he dispatched him to Bologna to be brought up there, like the little girl. What the lady said and showed in her face was no different from before, which stunned Gualtieri. He declared to himself that there wasn't a woman anywhere capable of behaving like that. If he hadn't seen her visceral attachment to the children as long as she had his approval, he would have thought she was glad to see the back of them, but he knew that there was sense and wisdom in her.

His subjects, believing he had had his children killed, strongly condemned him for his cruelty and felt nothing but compassion for the lady. When other ladies sympathized with her for having lost her children in this way, she said only that what pleased her was precisely what pleased the man who had fathered them.

Some years after the little girl's birth, Gualtieri decided it was time to put her capacity for endurance to the ultimate test. He told many of his men that he just could not bear Griselda being his wife any more, and that it was clear to him that marrying her had been a bad juvenile error; he was now going to do all he could to obtain special dispensation from the Pope to take another wife and leave Griselda. Quite a few of his better men took him to task, but he only replied that that was how things had to be. When his lady heard the news, she found herself having to face the idea of going back to her father's house, and perhaps tending the sheep as she had done in the past, with the added prospect of some other lady taking possession of the man to whom she had given all the love she had. She was devastated. But she had borne all the other wrongs that fortune had done her, and she set herself to bear this one with similar fortitude.

A little later Gualtieri arranged for some counterfeit letters to be sent from Rome and gave his subjects to believe that in these the Pope had given him dispensation to marry again and leave Griselda. He had her summoned and addressed her before a crowd of onlookers.

'My lady,' he said, 'thanks to a special concession granted me by the Pope, I can take another wife and let you go. Since my ancestors were from the high nobility and the lords of these lands, whereas yours have always been labourers, I intend that you should no longer be my wife and should go back to Giannucolo's house with the dowry you brought me. After that I shall marry someone I've found who will be appropriate for my station.'

Hearing this, the lady had to make an immense effort, one beyond women's natural capacities, in order to keep back her tears.

'My lord,' she replied, 'I always knew my lowly origins in no way accorded with your own nobility. I was glad to attribute to God and to yourself the position I have enjoyed with you. I have never thought it something I had been given, or treated it as anything more than a loan. Your wish is to recover it. I must make it my wish to let you have it, and I am happy to do so. Here is the ring with which you married me. Take it. You order me to carry away with me the dowry I brought you. That's not something for which you'll need a banker, or for which I'll need a bag or a packhorse. It does not escape me that you took me in naked. If you consider it decent for that body in which I carried the children you fathered to be seen by all and sundry, I shall go away naked. But I beg you that you let me have some payment for the virginity that I brought here and do not take away again by allowing me, over and above my dowry, to have a single shift to wear.'

Gualtieri wanted to weep more than anything else. But his face stayed as hard as ever.

'So you go off with a shift then,' he said.

Everyone round him begged him to make her the gift of a robe, and not let the woman who had been his wife for thirteen years or more be seen leaving his house penniless and utterly humiliated, which was what leaving in just a shift would mean. But their requests came to nothing. So it was in a shift, barefoot and bareheaded, that the lady commended them to God's care, and walked out of her husband's house and back to her father's, amid the weeping and wailing of all who saw her.

Giannucolo had never been able to believe that Gualtieri really wanted his daughter as his wife, expecting every day something like this to happen, and had kept the clothes she was wearing on the morning Gualtieri married her. He brought them out and she put them on. Then she gave herself over to the menial tasks around her father's house that she used to do in the past, valiantly bearing the savage assault that hostile fortune had inflicted on her.

Gualtieri's next step was to pretend to his subjects that he had got himself a daughter of one of the Counts of Panago. In the course of the grandiose preparations for the marriage ceremony, he sent for Griselda to come and see him.

'I'm bringing here as my bride,' he said to her when she arrived, 'this lady I've very recently promised to marry. My intention is to receive her with due honour when she comes here for the first time. You're aware that I don't have ladies in the house who can spruce up the rooms and do all the things required for a festive occasion of this sort. Since you know better than anyone else how this house works, sort out what needs to be done, and also invite a welcome party of ladies you think suitable, and receive them as if you were the lady in charge. Then once the marriage-feast is over, you can go back to your own house.'

His words were so many knives in Griselda's heart. She had never been able to abandon the love she felt for him in the way she had let go of her good fortune.

'My lord, I am willing and ready,' she said.

And so, in a makeshift dress of thick, rough cloth, she went back into the house she had left in just her shift not long before, and began sweeping the chambers and tidying them up, fixing hangings and drapes in the halls, and getting the kitchen ready, doing every single thing with her own hands as if she were nothing but a mere servant-girl. Nor did she stop till she had everything as neat and orderly as the occasion required.

Once she had had invitations sent out on Gualtieri's behalf to all the ladies in the area, the only thing left for her to do was to await the coming festivities. When the day of the wedding-feast arrived, in spite of the poor clothes she had on, she gave every one of the ladies who came a joyful and dignified welcome.

Gualtieri had taken care the children should be properly

brought up in Bologna by his female relative, who had married into the house of the Counts of Panago. The girl was now twelve and the prettiest creature ever, and the boy was six. Gualtieri had written to the relative's husband, asking him to be so good as to bring his daughter and son to Saluzzo, accompanied by an appropriate guard of honour, and to tell everyone that he was bringing the girl to be Gualtieri's wife, with no hint to anyone of who she really was.

This gentleman did as the Marquis asked and set off with the girl, her brother and the guard of honour. After some days, around the time of the morning meal, they arrived in Saluzzo, where they found all the local people and many others from round about waiting for this new bride of Gualtieri. The girl was greeted by the ladies and entered the hall where the tables were laid out. Griselda, dressed just as she was, went towards her happily enough, saying, 'My lady is welcome.'

The other ladies, who had repeatedly but fruitlessly begged Gualtieri either to let Griselda stay in one of the chambers or to lend her one of the robes that were once hers, so that she would not appear before the visitors looking as she did, were now assigned their places at the tables and began to be served. The girl was the object of everybody's attention and the general view was that Gualtieri had made a good exchange. One of those who was most lavish with her praises, both of the girl and of her little brother, was Griselda.

Gualtieri thought he had now had all the proof he could want of the patience of his lady. He could tell that it was not at all affected by events, no matter how bizarre they were, and, given the wisdom he knew was in her, he was sure that dullness of mind was not a factor. He decided it was time to release her from the tortures he judged she must be suffering beneath her calm and steady exterior. He had her come forward and, before everyone who was there, gave her a smile and asked:

'What do you think of our bride?'

'My lord,' replied Griselda, 'I can only think very well of her. If her good sense is equal to her beauty, as I believe it must be, I have no doubt that living with her will make you the most most contented lord in the world. But I beg you with all my heart not to inflict on her the sort of wounds you inflicted on the other one, the one who was your wife before. I can't really believe that she could stand it. She's younger, and what's more she's been brought up in luxury, whereas the other had spent her childhood doing hard physical work.'

Gualtieri could see that she firmly believed that the girl was going to be his wife and yet still said nothing he could disapprove of. He sat her down at his side and then spoke.

'Griselda,' he said, 'it is now time for you to taste the fruit of your steadfast patience and for those who judged me cruel, unjust and inhuman to acknowledge that what I did had a deliberate purpose. I wanted to teach you to be a wife, to teach my critics how to take a wife and to keep one, and to bring about for myself unbroken peace and quiet for as long as my life with you might last. This was something I was very afraid wouldn't happen when I first took a wife. It was to test if it were possible that I inflicted on you the wounds and torments you are all too aware of.

'Since I have never perceived you going against my wishes in anything you have said or done, I judge that I do indeed have from you the contentment I desired. I therefore intend to restore to you in one single moment what I took from you over the years, and to apply the sweetest possible medicine to the wounds I inflicted. So now, with joy in your heart, receive this girl you think is my bride, and her brother too. These are our children that you and many others have long thought I had brutally murdered. And I myself am your husband, who loves you more than anything else. I think I can rightly and honestly boast that no other man alive can be as happy with his wife as I am.'

After this speech he put his arms round her and kissed her. He then raised her to her feet and led her, weeping for joy, over to where their daughter was sitting, astounded by what she was hearing. They tenderly embraced the two children, and then told the girl and many other people there the truth of the situation. The ladies were delighted to get up from the tables and go with Griselda into one of the chambers. Expressing hopes of a better outcome this time, they helped her out of her rough clothing and dressed her in one of her noble robes. Then they led her back into the hall a courtly lady, which even in her rags she had retained the air of being. There followed a moment of marvellous celebration with the children, and everyone showed their joy at the way things had turned out. Then they plunged into fun and merrymaking, which went on for days.

Everyone judged Gualtieri to have shown great wisdom, though they judged the tests inflicted on his lady to have been too severe, indeed intolerable. Griselda they held to have shown more wisdom than anyone.

After some days the Count of Panago returned to Bologna and Gualtieri took Giannucolo away from his work. From then he was treated as a proper father-in-law, and lived very happily and much respected until a ripe old age. After finding a noble husband for his daughter, Gualtieri himself lived a long and happy life with Griselda, and treated her with all possible honour.

What can be said here except that divine spirits descend from heaven even into poor houses and into royal houses come spirits which deserve more to look after pigs than be lords over men? Who else but Griselda could have borne the callous, unprecedented tests Gualtieri subjected her to, not just without tears but with what looked like cheerfulness? Perhaps it would have served him right if the woman he happened to pick had let another man shake her muff when she was driven from home in her shift, and that way got herself a decent dress.